This book is for Jayme, Sarah, Baby Renee... and their Moms..........

Published by Modern Publishing
A Division of Unisystems, Inc.

Printed in Spain

Here Comes Punkin

by Guy Gilchrist

MODERN PUBLISHING
A Division of Unisystems, Inc.
New York, N.Y. 10022

Here I come! My name is Punkin and I'm a baby. I like being a baby because I have my own special baby toys, baby books . . .

. . . baby booties . . .

. . . and baby clothes!

And when I want someone to give me something, I have my own special baby way of getting it.

I just let out a great big baby "WAAAAAH!"
That gets my whole family running.

I "WAAAAAH" for my doll!

I "WAAAAAH" for my teddy bear!

I "WAAAAAH"
when I'm hungry . . .

and
when I'm
lonely!

I may be little, but my
"WAAAAAH" is big.

It's the best thing about this baby business . . .
it even helps me get around.

Some babies crawl all over and get their knees dirty,
but not me . . .

I just "WAAAAAH!"

That's my ticket on the Mommy Express!

One loud "WAAAAAH" and the Mommy Express
takes me to my playpen . . .

to my baby swing . . .

or to the kitchen
for a bottle of juice.

But wait a minute! This isn't a bottle of juice.
It's baby food . . . MASHED CARROTS
and STRAINED PEACHES! *Yuck!*

My "WAAAAAH" has let me down!

My brother Mudpie laughs at me while he eats pizza and peanut butter and jelly sandwiches.

I let out an "I want pizza WAAAAAH" and throw
my baby food on the floor!

Mommy says I am a bad girl and that I have to eat mashed carrots and strained peaches until I get my baby teeth.

So how do I get baby teeth anyway? Do I send away for them in the mail? Can I get them for my birthday? Will the Tooth Fairy give them to me?

I know the Tooth Fairy leaves money under Mudpie's pillow when he loses a tooth. Maybe it works the *other* way too!

I'm going to leave money under my pillow and maybe the Tooth Fairy will leave baby teeth for me.

As soon as I get my baby teeth, I'm going to have a
pizza delivered for the Tooth Fairy and me!

And what if the Tooth Fairy *doesn't* bring me baby teeth and I'm stuck eating mashed carrots and strained peaches?

I'll just "WAAAAAH" louder than ever!
That should wake up the Tooth Fairy . . .
and everyone else in the neighborhood too!